THE *JEWEL OF THE SEA* CRUISE
by Susan Korman

Illustrations by
Gabriel Picart

Spot Illustrations by
Rich Grote

MAGIC ATTIC PRESS

J
Kor

Published by Magic Attic Press.

For more information contact:
Book Editor, Magic Attic Press, 866 Spring Street,
Westbrook, ME 04092-3808

First Edition
Printed in the United States of America
1 2 3 4 5 6 7 8 9 10

Magic Attic Club® is a registered trademark.

Christine E. Taylor, Publisher
Cindy Lawhorn, Art Director
Debra DeForte, Managing Editor

Edited by Judit Bodnar
Designed by Cindy Lawhorn

Korman, Susan
The Jewel of the Sea Cruise / by Susan Korman
Illustrations by Gabriel Picart, spot illustrations by Rich Grote
(Magic Attic Club)
Summary: All of the Magic Attic Club—Heather, Megan, Keisha, Alison and Rose—
find themselves on an exciting Caribbean cruise on a beautiful ship named Jewel of the Sea.
Dressed in fancy party dresses, the girls meet a stand-offish young girl from England
named Lady Ashley. When they find Lady Ashley crying in her state room, they
discover her secret. Can the girls come up with a plan in time to surprise Ashley
on her special day?
ISBN 1-57513-150-1 (hardback) ISBN 1-57513-149-8 (paperback)
ISBN 1-57513-151-X (library edition hardback)

As members of the
MAGIC ATTIC CLUB,
we promise to
be best friends,
share all of our adventures in the attic,
use our imaginations,
have lots of fun together,
and remember—the real magic is in us.

Alison   Keisha

Heather   Megan

Rose

Table of Contents

Prologue

When Alison, Heather, Keisha, and Megan find a
golden key buried in the snow, they have no idea that it
will change their lives forever. They discover that it
belongs to Ellie Goodwin, the owner of an old Victorian
house across the street from Alison's. Ellie, grateful when
they return the key to her, invites the girls to play in her
attic. There they find a steamer trunk filled with wonderful
outfits—party dresses, a princess gown, a ballet tutu,
cowgirl clothes, and many, many, more. The girls try on
some of the costumes and admire their reflections in a
tall, gilded mirror nearby. Suddenly they are transported
to a new time and place, embarking on the greatest
adventure of their lives.

After they return to the present and Ellie's attic,
they form the Magic Attic Club, promising to tell
each other every exciting detail of their future
adventures. Then they meet Rose Hopkins, a new
girl at school, and invite her to join the club and
share their amazing secret.

Chapter One

TAKING CARE OF MONTY

When will Ellie be back from her trip, Megan?" Rose Hopkins asked. It was a warm Saturday afternoon in May. Rose kicked her new red-and-white soccer ball along as she and her best friends walked to Ellie Goodwin's house.

"She's coming back Tuesday," Megan Ryder told Rose. She reached into the back pocket of her yellow skirt and pulled out a folded sheet of paper. "She left us a note with instructions about what we're supposed to do while she's away."

"Could I see it, Megan?" asked Keisha Vance.

"Sure." Megan handed it over.

Keisha unfolded the note, then read it aloud to the others.

> *Dear Girls,*
>
> *Thank you for agreeing to take care of Monty while I'm away. I'm sure he'll be glad to have your company! Please walk him twice a day: once in the morning, and once in the evening. I left dog food on the kitchen counter—he usually eats one can at five o'clock. You can leave the mail and any messages on the table in the kitchen.*
>
> *Thanks again! I'll see you on Tuesday afternoon.*
>
> Love,
Ellie

Keisha looked at the other girls, a bright smile lighting up her face. "There's something else," she told her friends. "P.S. In case you decide to visit the attic, the key is in its usual spot."

The five members of the Magic Attic Club loved spending time in Ellie's attic. The spacious upstairs room contained all kinds of interesting treasures—antiques, old magazine and newspaper clippings, tattered photos, and dozens of mementos from Ellie's travels around the world.

The girls' favorite thing in the attic was an old steamer trunk that held dozens of outfits. Whenever they tried on something from the trunk and stood in front of Ellie's special mirror, they soon found themselves whisked away to a faraway place for an exciting adventure.

"Where did Ellie go, anyway?" Heather Hardin asked, pushing her long brown hair behind one shoulder.

"She went to Nantucket Island with her friend Isabel," Megan replied. "She told me that they're staying at a historic inn that's over two hundred years old. Doesn't that sound cool?" she added.

Keisha nodded and smiled. Megan's enthusiasm didn't surprise her. She knew how much Megan loved to read, and lately she had been reading lots of historical books about colonial times. It was no wonder that she was intrigued by the idea of staying at a historic inn.

"I went to Nantucket last year with my family. We went whale watching and fishing," Alison McCann said, adjusting the brim of her black Philadelphia Flyers cap. Her blue eyes sparkling with mischief, she added, "My brothers were furious because I caught three fish, and they didn't catch any!"

The others laughed. They always enjoyed hearing

about her ongoing battles with her three brothers.

A moment later, the girls reached the white picket fence in front of Ellie's house. The flower beds in front were bursting with bold red tulips and cheerful daffodils. As the girls turned up the front walk, a familiar sound rang out.

"Yip! Yip! Yip!"

Rose smiled. "I think Monty knows it's time for his walk!"

Megan fished the house key out of her pocket. As the girls let themselves into the house, Ellie's West Highland terrier immediately bounded toward them. He wriggled with pleasure as Heather and Alison kneeled to pet him.

"Hello, Monty," Heather greeted him. "Are you lonely without Ellie here?"

The dog wagged his tail and covered her face with slobbery kisses.

"I think that means *yes* in terrier language, Heather," Keisha said, laughing.

Monty's leash hung from a peg near the front hall. Rose clipped it onto his collar, and the girls set out for a long walk through the neighborhood. When they were sure they'd tired out the little dog, they headed back to Ellie's. On the way in, Megan reached into the mailbox.

"Look at all the cards that came for Ellie," she said to Heather. In the kitchen, she riffled through the stack of catalogs and letters.

"Megan!" Alison teased her. "Ellie asked us to bring in her mail, not snoop through it!"

Megan felt her cheeks flush as Rose eyed the assortment of colorful envelopes on top of the pile.

"She's right, though," she said. "There are a lot of cards here."

Suddenly, something occurred to Rose. "When is Ellie's birthday?" she asked her friends.

"I don't know," Megan replied, setting the mail on the table.

"Me neither," Keisha admitted.

"I'll check her calendar," Alison said, jumping up to look at the large wall calendar on the refrigerator. "It doesn't mention her birthday," she reported a second later.

"Grownups never write down their own birthdays," Heather said. "My mom and dad usually want us to forget theirs!"

Keisha looked at her friends. "Well, if it is Ellie's birthday, we've got to do something for her. She's always so generous to us."

"I know," Megan agreed. "Last year on my birthday, she gave me a gift certificate to *The Book Exchange*."

"She sent me a bouquet of balloons for my birthday," Rose said.

Alison was about to tell her friends about the necklace Ellie had given her when the phone rang.

The girls looked at each other, unsure what to do.

"Should we get it?" Rose asked.

It rang again, and Heather shrugged. "Sure. We can take a message for her."

Rose was closest to the phone. "Hello?"

The man on the other end sounded surprised to hear an unfamiliar voice.

"Is this Ellie Goodwin's house?" he asked.

"Yes, but Ellie isn't home right now," Rose replied. "This is her neighbor, Rose Hopkins. May I take a message for her?"

"Please do," the man answered. "My name is Stan Eckstein. I'm one of Ellie's piano students, and I'm calling to see if she's planning to teach on Tuesday night."

"I'm not sure, but..." Rose motioned for Megan to pass her a pencil and sheet of paper. "I'll ask her to let you know."

The man gave Rose his phone number. "Please tell her that I was double-checking because that's her birthday."

"Her birthday?" Rose echoed.

"That's right," Mr. Eckstein said. "Ellie's birthday is May sixteenth."

"Are you sure, Mr. Eckstein?"

"I'm quite certain, young lady," he said with a chuckle. "It's my birthday, too."

"Thanks, Mr. Eckstein. I'll see that Ellie gets your message." Rose hung up and beamed at her friends. "Guess what?"

"What?" Heather said, noticing her satisfied grin.

"That was one of Ellie's music students," Rose reported. "And he told me that Ellie's birthday is the sixteenth!"

Megan glanced at the calendar. "That's this Tuesday."

"Let's put on our thinking caps, everybody," Heather said eagerly. "We're going to make sure that this is Ellie's best birthday ever!"

Chapter Two

A VISIT TO THE ATTIC

I've got it!" Heather said, snapping her fingers. "We can get Ellie a toaster. I know she needs one—hers broke a few weeks ago."

"A toaster?" Keisha wrinkled her nose. She didn't want to hurt Heather's feelings, but a new toaster wasn't exactly her idea of a fun birthday present.

"I don't know, Heather," Megan said, as if speaking Keisha's thoughts. "I'd like to come up with something more exciting than a toaster."

"How about a new address book and some stationery?" Rose suggested.

The others thought over the suggestion for a minute. Ellie had traveled all over the world and she had lots of friends who lived far away, but…

"That's sort of boring, too," Heather decided with a sigh.

After an hour the girls still hadn't come up with any good ideas.

"I know!" Alison suddenly shot up from her chair. "I've got a great idea!"

"Uh-oh!" Keisha said with a grin. "I've seen that look before, Ali. And it usually means trouble!"

Alison was so excited, she didn't hear Keisha teasing her.

"Let's throw a big surprise party for Ellie!" she went on. "That's what my mom did when my dad turned forty last year. She had it at the Oakview Country Club, and she invited about seventy-five people. Dad had a fabulous time."

"That *is* a good idea, Ali!" Megan said.

"Alison, you're a genius!" Heather proclaimed.

"Let's see…" Keisha was already planning the guest list. "Ellie has so many friends. We should invite our parents; and Mr. Newman, Ellie's friend who owns *The Book Exchange*; and then, there are her music students…"

Heather tore two sheets of paper from the pad in front of Rose. *Guests*, she wrote at the top of one page. On the next sheet of paper, she wrote *Things to Do*.

Alison took charge. "The first thing we have to do is choose a date," she said. "Then we have to call the country club to see if it's available for that date."

Heather wrote those things down. "What else, Ali?"

"We'll definitely need a cake. I'm sure my mom would help us with something, if the country club doesn't supply one. Desserts are her specialty. Having a caterer in the family comes in handy sometimes."

"Write down decorations and invitations, too, Heather," Keisha said.

"We have to get elegant decorations," Heather said. "I don't want this to be like a kids' party with balloons and a clown and that kind of stuff."

"Hey!" Alison's eyes lit up with another idea. "Maybe we can ask the country club if they can make one of those fancy ice sculptures. Have you guys ever seen them?"

"I have," Keisha said. "My cousin had an ice sculpture of two swans at her wedding reception last year. It was so cool."

"So cool?" Alison said, giggling. Keisha looked at her, puzzled.

"Get it?" Alison explained. "The *ice* sculptures were *cool*?"

"Very funny," Keisha said, making a face at Alison's corny joke.

Keisha and Megan made a few more suggestions about decorations. Heather wrote them down, then looked at Rose.

"You're so quiet, Rose."

Rose hesitated for a second.

I hate to be a party pooper, you guys," she said slowly, "but I think we're forgetting something."

"We've got decorations, invitations, ice sculptures, fresh flowers, candles, and present," Heather said, looking at her lists. "What did we forget?"

"Money," Rose said flatly. "A party at Oakview Country Club is going to cost a fortune."

The room went silent as Rose's words sank in.

"I have some money saved up," Alison murmured finally.

"How much?" Rose asked.

"Thirty-four dollars and fifty-nine cents," Alison answered. "It's not a lot, but it's a start."

"I have about twelve dollars," Keisha said.

Megan did some quick calculations on the sheet of paper in front of Heather.

"That's forty-six dollars and fifty-nine cents," she announced. "Plus, I have about forty dollars myself. That's almost ninety dollars."

"I'm completely broke," Heather said apologetically.

"Me, too," Rose said.

"That's not even close to what we'll need for a party at the country club," Keisha said with a sigh. Dejected, she propped her elbows on the kitchen table.

Megan stood to get a drink of water. "Maybe we could have the party at my house," she said, thinking aloud. "If we do the work and pay for everything, I think my mom wouldn't mind."

"We still don't have enough money," Rose reminded her. "Remember? We need invitations, decorations, a cake, a present..." She ticked off the items on her fingers.

"We can make everything ourselves," Keisha suggested.

"But we want this to be an elegant party," Heather said. The others nodded glumly.

"Come on, you guys," Rose said, feeling bad that she'd been the one to bring up the subject of money. "We're the Magic Attic Club—we can think of something."

Twenty minutes later, the girls still hadn't come up with another idea. After the thought of having a party at the country club, nothing else seemed right for a friend as special as Ellie.

"I have an idea," Rose said at last. "But it's not about

Ellie's birthday," she added as her friends looked at her hopefully. "Why don't we visit the attic?"

Alison's face instantly brightened. "That's the best idea any of us has had all day, Rose!" she said. "Come on, you guys!"

Monty was lying on the kitchen floor. As the girls jumped up from the table, he thumped his tail a few times, but didn't bother to lift his head.

"See you later, Monty," Heather said to the sleepy dog. "We're going upstairs."

Megan stepped into the attic and reached for the tasseled cord that hung from the overhead lamp. As the light flicked on, Megan took a quick look around the room—even though by now she knew every inch of the place by heart.

Near one corner stood an antique desk stuffed with old letters and scrapbooks. To her right was a tall mahogany wardrobe with hat boxes piled on top. A worn Oriental rug covered part of the floor, and the room smelled faintly sweet, like cedar mingled with lavender.

Keisha and Heather were already lifting the lid of the large, black leather and oak steamer trunk.

A long, old-fashioned dress caught Heather's eye. With

its full skirt and petticoats, it reminded her of the Southern ladies' gowns in *Gone with the Wind*.

"These are neat," Alison said, picking up a pair of chunky white goggles and trying them on.

"You look like Amelia Earhart, the famous aviator, Alison," Megan told her.

Keisha was on her knees, eagerly sorting through the things inside the trunk. Suddenly, she noticed a pretty lavender fabric. Pulling it out, Keisha realized that it was a sleeveless dress with white polka dots and a white lace collar.

"Isn't this beautiful?" she said, holding it up under her chin so her friends could see.

"You look ready for a fancy party, Keisha," Rose told her.

"Are there any more party dresses in there?" Heather asked hopefully.

Megan was already rummaging inside. Within minutes, she had found a pink and white checked dress with short, puffy sleeves for Heather and a green and white dress with a sheer lacy skirt for Rose.

Alison pulled out a two-piece blue outfit spangled with white stars. "Dibs on this one!" she said.

Megan had set aside a dress that she wanted to wear. It was pale yellow—her favorite color—with soft, full sleeves and a pretty flower appliqué on the front.

Keisha and the others had already changed. Now they

were standing in front of the tall, gilded mirror.

"Come on, Megan," Keisha waved her over.

Megan kicked off her shoes and slipped the dress over her head. A moment later the five of them stared at their reflection.

"We look beautiful!" Rose said with a wide smile.

"Even if we say so ourselves!" Alison put in.

Megan closed her eyes, wondering where the mirror was about to take them.

Chapter
Three

THE JEWEL OF
THE SEA

s the scent of Ellie's attic faded, Rose felt a warm breeze brush her face.

"Where are we?" she murmured, looking around. To her surprise, it was nighttime and she and her friends stood outdoors under a dark sky. Before Rose could tell anything more, the floor under her feet suddenly lurched.

"Whoa!" Rose cried, reaching out a hand to steady herself on the wooden railing in front of her. When she looked down, all she saw was pitch-black water.

"Where are we?" Keisha said uneasily.

"I think we're on a boat," Megan said.

As Rose looked around, she realized that Megan was right—they stood at the prow of a big ship that was gliding through the water. Behind her was a rack of life preservers marked *Property of The Jewel of the Sea*.

"This must be a cruise ship," she said.

"Cool!" Alison said happily. "I've always wanted to go on a cruise. Maybe we'll—"

"Keisha! Megan! Rose!" a voice called.

Alison looked up to see two girls hurrying toward them. As they drew closer, she saw that one of them had dark hair and wore a sea-green dress with narrow straps. The other girl was taller, with long blond hair. She had on a bright yellow dress with a short, fluttery skirt.

The dark-haired girl put her hands on her hips and grinned.

"Where have you been?" she asked in a British accent. "Laura and I have been looking all over for you."

"Yes." The girl in the yellow dress spoke with a British accent, too. "Amy and I were beginning to worry that the five of you had been captured by pirates."

"Or that you had jumped into the Caribbean and swum all the way to Jamaica!" the girl named Amy joked.

Jamaica! Megan thought. *Is that where we are? Near the island of Jamaica?*

"Come on." Amy linked arms with Megan and quickly led her away from the prow and toward the middle of the deck. "We have to hurry. The ice cream social started ten minutes ago."

"And you know Mrs. Stonebridge," Laura added. "She's the strictest teacher at the academy. She's probably dispatched a search party to look for us by now!"

Megan wanted to ask Laura why they were all aboard the cruise ship and what academy she meant, but she stayed quiet. She knew she had to be careful not to reveal the secret of Ellie's attic.

Laura stopped at a bank of elevators and pushed a button.

"I still can't get over how beautiful the *Jewel of the Sea* is," Amy remarked while they waited for an elevator to arrive.

"I know," Laura agreed. "Or that it has nine decks and that every one of them is named after a gemstone."

"Where's the ice cream social being held?" Keisha asked.

"On the Emerald Deck, in the Diamond Room," Laura answered. "My favorite swimming pools are here, on the

Sapphire Deck."

Pools? With an S? Heather thought, amazed. She'd never been aboard a luxury ocean liner before, and she couldn't believe how enormous this one was. When they got off the elevator on the Emerald Deck, she spotted signs pointing to a movie theater, a health and fitness center, a card room, even a library!

"I'm glad we bumped into Laura and Amy," Megan whispered in her ear. "At least *they* know their way around this ship!"

Heather nodded her agreement. As they approached the Diamond Room, she heard kids laughing and music blaring. When she and her friends entered the room, several others greeted them. On the dance floor, small groups of girls were dancing to a fast song. As Heather listened to them talking, she realized that most were British, like Laura and Amy; a few others sounded American.

A tall, prim-looking woman raised her eyebrows as Heather and the girls approached.

"I'm glad you could join the Wilshire Academy contingent, ladies," she said tartly.

"Sorry we're late, Mrs. Stonebridge," Amy said quickly. "It took us a long while to get dressed for the party."

"Hmmm..." The chaperon sniffed. "Please make sure it doesn't happen again."

Amy seemed eager to change the subject.
"Is there any ice cream left, Ms. Clarke?" she asked the woman beside Mrs. Stonebridge. Heather noticed that this teacher was younger with a stylish haircut and friendly blue eyes.

"I don't think they ever run out of food on this ship!" Ms. Clarke replied with a smile. She pointed to a long table at the far end of the room. "The ice cream is over there, where Ashley Worthingham is standing. After you have yours, you can mingle with the other students. You should get to know some girls here from the London boarding schools, as well as the ones from the States."

Alison got in line behind Ashley, the girl Ms. Clarke had pointed out. Two waiters, dressed in black jackets, bow ties, and crisp white shirts, were serving the ice cream.

"Here you go, miss." One man handed Alison a tall, elegant-looking sundae dish heaped with vanilla and chocolate ice cream. His gold name tag read "Roger."

"The syrups and toppings are at the other end of the table," Roger told Alison with a smile.

Alison ladled butterscotch syrup generously onto her ice cream, then moved down to the selection of toppings. To her delight, there were nuts, miniature marshmallows, fresh berries, whipped cream, sprinkles, and a dozen different types of candies in a rainbow of colors.

"Wow," Alison said to Ashley. "I've never been to an ice cream social before, but so far this one is great."

Ashley turned around. She was tall and wore a pink lace dress with a matching bow clipped to her blond hair. She was very pretty, but to Alison's surprise, her expression wasn't the least bit friendly.

"I suppose some people might find this fun," she said coldly. "Personally, I think ice cream socials are rather juvenile." With that, she turned back to the dessert table.

Rather juvenile? Alison thought indignantly. *Well, excuse me for acting like a kindergartner!*

Alison was still simmering when she had finished concocting her sundae and carried it to an empty table. As soon as her friends joined her, she told them about Ashley's snide remark.

Megan shrugged. "We just got here," she reminded Alison. "Maybe something happened that we don't know about."

Keisha nodded. "Don't let that girl bother you, Ali. She probably didn't mean to be rude."

Alison knew her friends were right, but she still had trouble letting go of her hurt feelings.

"Well, I thought people were supposed to be *sociable* at an ice cream social," she grumbled, digging her spoon into her sundae.

A few minutes later, Laura and Amy joined them. While

the girls ate their ice cream, the two British students
entertained them with funny stories about pranks they'd
played on students and teachers at Wilshire Academy.

"Remember the time we told Hillary that the Queen
Mum was my godmother?" Laura said to Amy.

Amy nodded, her blue eyes twinkling merrily.

"Who's the Queen Mum?" Heather blurted out,
forgetting that she was probably expected to know this.

Amy gave her a quizzical look. "She's the Queen's
mother, of course."

"It was a brilliant scheme," Laura said, returning to the

topic of their prank. "For months, Hillary thought I was a dear friend of the royal family. She's an American, too," she went on, laughing, "and she thought she had to curtsy every time she saw me!"

Rose laughed. "What other stunts have you two pulled?"

"One of my favorites was the faculty tea caper," Amy said. "Right before the tea, Laura and I sneaked into the kitchen and replaced all the hard-boiled eggs with uncooked ones."

"Uh-oh," Megan said, grinning.

"You should have seen Mrs. Stonebridge's face when she tried to peel her egg," Laura chimed in. "It cracked open, right onto her plate!"

Soon Alison was laughing so hard at Laura's and Amy's mischief that tears spilled down her cheeks. By the time she'd polished off her ice cream and stood up to dance, her good mood had returned.

Nothing cheered her up faster than a funny story— except for a butterscotch sundae.

A short while later, the Magic Attic Club girls and the other students from Wilshire Academy made their way to their rooms for the night. Luckily, Megan had managed to peek at Ms. Clarke's clipboard during the evening so she knew their room assignments.

"We're in rooms five-oh-six-nine and five-oh-six-seven," she whispered to her friends as they stepped off the elevator onto the Ruby Deck.

Megan, Rose, and Heather were assigned to one room while Alison and Keisha bunked next door. The girls discovered that each of the state rooms had two large beds and two dressers, plus a small bathroom and sitting area. To their delight, a door connected the two rooms.

After they'd finished exploring their sleeping quarters, the girls decided they were ready to go to bed.

"Night, you guys," Megan said to Alison and Keisha as they stood up to go.

"See you in the morning," Keisha and Alison called back, closing the door behind them.

Megan hung up the yellow party dress, then slipped on a night shirt from one of the dresser drawers.

"I'm soooo tired," she told Rose and Heather.

"Me, too," Rose agreed. She had already climbed into bed next to Heather and was brushing out her long black hair.

"I'm having such a good time," Heather said happily. "Amy and Laura are really nice, and I love—"

Just then a shriek cut her off.

Heather bolted up in bed as another scream ripped through the air.

Oh no! she thought. The screams were coming from next door!

Chapter
Four

"JAMAICA! JAMAICA!"

That's Alison and Keisha!" Heather exclaimed. She leaped out of bed and raced for the door between the two rooms.

Rose was right behind her as Heather threw open the door. For a second, Rose held her breath, scared to look inside.

But to her surprise, Alison and Keisha didn't look like two girls who'd just screamed in fright. Instead the two of them were sitting on Keisha's bed, laughing hysterically.

Rose put her hands on her hips. "What's so funny, you two?" Alison was laughing so hard, she could barely talk. "Ants…" was all she could manage. "There are ants…"

"Come on, you guys," Megan said impatiently. "Tell us why you're laughing."

It took Alison and Keisha several minutes to calm down.

"Look!" Keisha said, peeling back the bed covers.

Heather gasped. Huge swarms of tiny black ants were outlined against the pale sheets.

"Gross!" Rose cried, jumping back.

Alison and Keisha burst out laughing again. "They're plastic!" Keisha managed to inform them.

"Somebody played a joke on us," Alison added, "and I'll give you one guess who did it!"

"Laura and Amy!" Heather said.

"So that's why they left the ice cream social early," Megan mused out loud. "They wanted to sneak up here to leave you a little present."

"Well, those two don't know who they're messing with," Alison said with a grin. "As soon as I think of a good plan, I'm going to get revenge."

The girls were still laughing about Laura and Amy's prank when a sharp rap sounded on the door.

The five of them exchanged nervous looks.

"Yes?" Keisha called.

The door opened, and Ms. Clarke peered inside. "Is everything all right, girls?" she asked, frowning.

"Yes, Ms. Clarke," Megan answered quickly. "We were just talking."

"Well, it's a bit late for chit-chat," the chaperon said sternly. "Heather, Megan, and Rose, please return to your room at once. I want all of you to turn out the lights and go to sleep."

"Yes, Ms. Clarke," Keisha said.

Yikes! Heather thought as she, Rose, and Megan jumped off Keisha's bed and scurried back to their own room. *We've only been on board the ship for a few hours, and the chaperons have already scolded us twice.*

As she slid under the cool sheets, she decided that the Magic Attic Club had better be a little more careful tomorrow—especially around that strict Mrs. Stonebridge.

After breakfast the students from Wilshire Academy assembled in the Garnet Lounge so that Mrs. Stonebridge and Ms. Clarke could tell them the plans for the day.

"Please sit down, girls," Mrs. Stonebridge called, clapping her hands. Keisha checked out the group as she waited for everyone to settle down. Last night, at the ice cream social, she hadn't been able to tell which girls were from Wilshire Academy and which were from other schools. Now she recognized Ashley Worthingham, as well as Laura and Amy and about fifteen other girls from the academy.

Mrs. Stonebridge clapped again loudly to get everyone's attention.

"Later this morning, some of us will participate in today's excursion to Jamaica," she began. "I'm sure that all of you know that this island was formerly a colony of Great Britain. Now, who can tell me when Jamaica was granted her independence?"

A girl with red hair raised her hand. "Nineteen sixty-two, Mrs. Stonebridge."

"Excellent, Hillary. Now, the chief crops cultivated here are...?"

Laura, who was sitting next to Keisha, groaned softly. "I thought we were supposed to be on holiday," she said under her breath.

"Doesn't Mrs. Stonebridge *ever* relax and have fun?" Keisha asked.

"I don't think so," Laura whispered back as the teacher went on about bananas, nutmeg and sugarcane. "She seems to take everything very seriously."

"I'll say," Keisha muttered.

At last, Mrs. Stonebridge's lecture came to an end, and it was Ms. Clarke's turn to stand and address the students.

"When the ship stops, you may choose to go ashore for a few hours and tour the island," the younger chaperon explained. "Or you may stay on board and see a movie, or go swimming, or do whatever you like."

Keisha turned to her Magic Attic Club friends. "I want to go ashore!" she said eagerly.

"Me, too!" Rose said.

"Me, three!" Alison chimed in.

Heather and Megan wanted to go on the sightseeing excursion, too. But to Keisha's surprise, Laura and Amy said they were tired and wanted to stay aboard the ship to relax and take a nap.

"Speaking of sleep..." Amy cast a look at Keisha and Alison. "How did you two sleep last night?" she asked.

Keisha had to fight back her grin. Amy was obviously trying to find out what had happened when they found the plastic ants.

"Fine," Keisha replied, pretending to be puzzled. "Why?"

"We were just wondering," Laura said quickly.

"Right," Amy chimed in. "Sarah and Tricia said they got a little seasick last night."

"Well, not us," Alison said, playing along. "Keisha and I

slept as peacefully as little babies."

Keisha didn't dare look at Alison or any of her other best friends until Laura and Amy stood. But as soon as Laura and Amy left the lounge, the Magic Attic Club girls burst out laughing.

Eleven other girls from Wilshire had decided to go with Mrs. Stonebridge to Jamaica.

Megan had expected the big cruise ship to pull into a port and dock somewhere to let the passengers off. Instead, the *Jewel of the Sea* simply steered closer to the island, then stopped. Megan watched in surprise as several large motor boats sped toward the cruise ship. Mrs. Stonebridge explained that these smaller boats would ferry them to shore.

Megan took a life jacket from the helmsman, then jumped onto the boat behind Alison. The wind whipped her face as she gazed out at the sea.

Last night, when the five girls had arrived, the water had looked dark and opaque. Now, in the bright sunlight, the Caribbean Sea sparkled like a clear turquoise jewel. In the distance Megan could see Jamaica's rolling mountains, densely covered and green.

"It's beautiful!" She had to shout to be heard above the noise from the motor.

"I've never seen such blue water," Rose replied.

"Or such white sand!" Heather added, pointing to the beaches along the shoreline.

As the motorboat drew closer, the lively beat of reggae music filled the air. Megan saw four men playing musical instruments standing on the beach to welcome them. They were singing a song, which she recognized from the Olympic events she'd watched with Ali. It was the anthem, "Jamaica, Jamaica."

The motor boat was about fifty feet or so from the shore when the helmsman cut the engine. He tossed a rope to a tall Jamaican who began to tow them inshore.

As the boat reached the beach, the sweet scent of pineapples wafted out to greet them. All along the shore Megan could see bright red flowers blooming on lush green plants.

"Welcome to Jamaica!" a striking woman in a colorful skirt and blouse called in a lilting voice. She smiled warmly at Megan. "I hope you enjoy your visit to our beautiful island."

"I'm sure we will," Megan said, smiling back at her. She had already fallen in love with the beautiful island.

The first stop for the group was Dunns' River Falls with cascades six hundred feet high. The girls linked hands while a guide led them up limestone steps.

"Wow," Alison murmured, panting for breath when they reached the top of the waterfalls. "This is incredible!"

"It sure is," Keisha agreed. At several points below, the river cascaded into naturally terraced pools. Dozens of people splashed about in the warm blue hollows, shrieking with pleasure, as they stood under the streams of water. Keisha couldn't wait to join them!

After the stop at Dunns' River Falls, a bus took the girls to the town of Ochos Rios for lunch and shopping. Near the souvenir stands, Alison spotted three women weaving tourists' hair into long, beaded cornrows.

"Let's get our hair braided!" she said eagerly.

Her friends didn't need the least bit of convincing. They told Mrs. Stonebridge where they were going, then rushed over.

Alison was the first to sit down. She chatted with her friends and the weavers while the women plaited the girls' hair. Finally, the Jamaican woman held up a mirror so Alison could see the results.

"It looks great!" Alison declared happily. She swung her

head this way and that, loving the way the blue and white beads at the ends of her braids clacked together.

By the time all five girls' hair had been braided, it was time to meet the rest of their group. The girls spotted Ashley and Sarah sitting near a thatched hut. Inside, a local woman was selling jewelry, straw baskets, woven goods, and other island trinkets.

Sarah showed them the silver bangle bracelets she'd bought for her mother.

"They're not real silver or anything," she said. "But I think my mum will like them. I also bought some placemats for my grandparents."

Megan admired the red, woven placemats embroidered with intricate designs.

"They're pretty," she told Sarah with a smile. Then she turned to Ashley and asked, "Did you buy anything for your family?"

Ashley smirked. "I'm afraid my father wouldn't be very interested in the junk that's sold here."

"I thought they had some cool things," Sarah said defensively.

Ashley put on a syrupy smile. "I expect that *you're* used to shopping for souvenirs at little places like this."

Sarah's face flamed.

What a snob! Megan thought angrily. There had been no call for her to be so mean to Sarah. Megan wanted to say something back to Ashley, but just then Mrs. Stonebridge came up.

"Come along, girls," the teacher said briskly. "It's time to meet the ferries back at the beach."

As Megan stood up to follow the others, she felt Alison put a hand on her arm.

"Maybe we'll get lucky and Ashley will fall overboard on the way back to the ship," she murmured into Megan's ear.

Megan grimaced. Right now she was so furious, she almost felt like *shoving* Ashley overboard!

Chapter

Five

THE QUEENS OF THE SHUFFLEBOARD COURT

Alison pushed the red disk with her long stick, then watched it sail toward the opposite end of the shuffleboard court. The disk stopped neatly inside the box marked "10".

"Way to go, Alison!" Heather cheered. "We're eight points ahead of them now!"

"The game isn't over yet, you two," Amy teased them.

"That's right," Laura echoed with a grin. "Yesterday we beat Sarah and Courtney—*and* Mary and Beatrice. The stewards declared us 'Queens of the Shuffleboard Court!"

"Speaking of queens...," Heather began as she approached the line with her stick. "what in the world is Ashley's problem? She was so rude to Sarah yesterday." Quickly, she told Amy and Laura what Ashley had said.

The two girls exchanged a glance before Amy turned to Heather and stuck her nose in the air.

"Well, it's not everyone who's a real *lady*," she said, her British accent exaggeratedly nasal.

"What do you mean?" Alison asked.

"Didn't you know?" Laura piped up. "Her father is Earl Worthingham—the seventh Earl Worthingham, if you want to be exact."

"Really?" Heather said, looking from Laura to Amy.

"Of course," Amy said, stepping up to the line to take her turn at shuffleboard. "If you lived in England year-round, you'd know all about Earl Worthingham and the famous people with whom he takes his holidays."

"Lady Ashley herself often goes to Buckingham Palace for tea with the queen," Laura said.

"No way!" Alison burst out laughing. "You two are teasing us!"

"No, we're not," Amy said matter-of-factly. "Ashley and her father are, truly, members of the British aristocracy."

"Right," Alison muttered under her breath. "And my father is related to George Washington."

A few minutes later, Amy and Laura huddled together
to tally the scores.

"They're trying to trick us again," Alison muttered to
Heather. "Just like they fooled Hillary into thinking that
the Queen mum is Laura's godmother."

Before Heather could reply, Laura looked over at them.
"You two are still in the lead, but not for long," she
announced cheerfully.

The girls picked up their sticks and the colored disks,
then moved to the opposite end of the court.

"Oh, by the way," Amy said as they continued playing.
"We bumped into Ms. Clarke after lunch. She asked us to
tell you to wear your pajamas to dinner."

"Our pajamas?" Heather repeated in surprise.

Amy nodded. "The staff and crew are hosting a pajama
party tonight," she explained. "Afterward the captain's
going to tell us bedtime stories."

"Bedtime stories?" Alison echoed.

"Personally, I can't wait," Amy replied. "Won't it be fun
to see Mrs. Stonebridge in her nightie?" she added,
making them all giggle.

Keisha, Megan, and Rose were stretched out on
cushioned lounge chairs beside the diving pool, reading
magazines and sipping tall glasses of lemonade.

"Hi, guys," Alison said, hurrying over.

"Ali and I whomped the 'Queens of the Shuffleboard Court!'" Heather announced.

"You mean, Amy and Laura?" Megan asked, sitting up.

Alison nodded. "Only, those two are more like court jesters," she added, rolling her eyes. "They said we're supposed to call Ashley Worthingham '*Lady* Ashley' because her father is an earl."

"An earl?" Keisha repeated, raising her eyebrows skeptically. "That's a good one."

Just then Ms. Clarke walked up, carrying a beach towel. "Did Laura and Amy tell you about dressing up for dinner tonight?" she asked.

"They sure did," Heather answered.

"Good," the teacher replied. "It should be fun. I'll be there with my boots on," she added, then headed for the pool.

"Boots?" Alison giggled. "She wears boots with her pajamas?"

"Maybe it's some kind of British custom," Heather said, laughing.

"What in the world are you two talking about?" Rose asked.

"Sorry, guys," Alison apologized, and quickly told her friends about the pajama party.

Megan wrinkled her nose. "I was hoping dinner would be more formal tonight. I want to wear my party dress again."

"Me, too," Keisha said.

"Our adventure isn't over yet," Heather reminded them. "Maybe we'll get to wear them again soon."

"Those rabbit slippers are a perfect match with your nightshirt, Megan," Keisha said, pretending to admire her friend's dinner outfit. "Where in the world did you find them?"

"I bought them at one of the boutiques near the Diamond Room," Megan replied. She giggled as she spun around to model her nightshirt and the furry white bunny slippers on her feet. Keisha and Rose had on boxer shorts and T-shirts, while Heather wore a pair of striped pajamas—along with several curlers that she'd found in a drawer and haphazardly rolled into her hair.

"And I absolutely love your nightgown, Alison," Keisha went on. "The lobsters on it are so..." She searched for the right word.

"So *ugly*?" Alison finished for her.

"Exactly!" Keisha replied, laughing.

The girls went to the Topaz Deck, then straight to the Opal Suite.

"Country and Western," Keisha said, pushing open the door. "I like this song, but it's not exactly a lullaby."

As Rose followed Keisha into the room, she gasped in surprise. In front of her was a huge placard that read

Welcome to rodeo night at the Opal Corral. Red and white checkered cloths covered each table and fake tumbleweeds and cacti were scattered across the floor.

"*Rodeo* Night!" Alison shrieked when she read the sign. "I thought it was Pajama Night!"

Nearly everyone in the room was looking at them. Even Roger—who was dressed Western-style in jeans and a white shirt with a string tie—was laughing.

"Cute bunny slippers, Megan!" a familiar voice yelled.

Megan looked up to see Laura and Amy grinning and waving at her. She felt her face turn ten shades of red.

"I'm going to kill those two," she said through clenched teeth.

"You're not the only one," Alison chimed in.

"Let's get out of here, you guys," Rose said. She whirled around, and her friends followed.

"Laura and Amy did it again!" Heather declared as the girls rushed down the corridor.

By the time the girls had changed clothes and returned to the Opal Room, half the other kids had finished dinner. "Mmm-mmmm, my favorite," said Keisha, filling her plate with hot chili and all the fixings—rice, cheese, peppers,

and extra onions. Then she led the way to an unoccupied table.

"Me, too," Heather said. "And this lemon meringue pie looks *yummy*. Come on, Rose, try some."

"I've lost my appetite," Rose said. "I'm still too embarrassed about showing up in our PJs."

"We did look pretty ridiculous," Alison said, smiling ruefully. "But don't worry, Rose. The Magic Attic Club will get revenge!"

Suddenly Ashley Worthingham appeared at their table.

"Those curlers were a charming touch, Heather!" she

said. "And Megan's bunny slippers..." Ashley rolled her eyes.

Heather clamped her mouth shut and stabbed her fork into her pie. Her friends' tight-lipped expressions told her they felt the same way she did.

"Amy and Laura tricked us," Keisha began. "They said—"

Before she could finish, Ashley stood up and gave the girls a syrupy smile.

"Excuse me, ladies. I have something interesting to do now." She waggled her fingers at them and walked away.

Megan watched her go. "Is it me?" she asked, turning to her friend. "Or is Ashley Worthingham the most annoying person on the face of the earth?"

Chapter Six

LADY ASHLEY

O kay, here's the plan," Alison said. The corridor outside the girls' state rooms was quiet and deserted. "Rose and I will sneak into Laura and Amy's room. Everyone will be back soon, so you guys wait here and play lookout."

"Where'd you get the ammunition, Ali?" Keisha asked with a grin.

"From the kitchen," Alison replied. "There was a ton of whipped cream left over from the social, and I asked the staff if we could take some for a special project."

"A 'special project'?" Rose laughed. "Didn't they want to know what it was?"

"I grabbed these and tore out of the kitchen so fast, they didn't have time to ask me any questions," Alison confessed.

"Are you sure we won't damage anything?" Megan asked, worried. "I don't want Laura and Amy to get into big trouble."

"It'll be messy, but I promise, nothing will be ruined," Alison reassured her.

"Don't forget to set their alarms, too," Keisha reminded Alison and Rose. "We want a buzzer to go off every hour between three and seven AM."

"How are we going to get in?" Rose asked.

"Easy." Alison said, holding up a card key. "Hillary and Sarah's room connects with theirs. Believe me, after the tricks that Laura and Amy have played on them, they were thrilled to help."

Megan shook her head. "You're amazing, Ali. How in the world do you think of this stuff?"

Alison grinned proudly. "Living with three brothers has given me years of experience!"

A few minutes later, Rose and Alison made their way down the corridor, weapons in hand.

"First, we'll unscrew all the light bulbs so the lights

won't go on when they enter their room," Alison said. "Then, I'll set their alarm clocks, while you..."

Suddenly Rose thought she heard something—a choked, muffled noise. She stopped to listen.

"Did you hear that, Ali?" she asked in a whisper.

Alison turned around. "Hear what?"

"It sounds as if someone's crying," Rose said, still whispering. Glancing to her left, she noticed a door open a crack. Rose motioned for her friend to be quiet as she tiptoed closer. Carefully, she leaned toward the open door and peeked inside.

A girl was sitting on the bed, crying quietly.

Rose quickly ducked out of sight. "It's *Ashley!*" she whispered.

Alison peered into the state room to see for herself. "She looks pretty upset."

"What should we do?" Rose asked.

Alison shrugged. "I don't know. It's not as if we're her friends."

"But what if something is really wrong?" Rose said, worried. "Maybe we should ask if she's okay."

"Why? So she can bite our heads off again?" Alison said.

As she leaned around Rose to get another look, her

arm bumped the door frame.

"Watch it, Ali!" Rose whispered frantically. But it was too late. A can Alison had been carrying dropped to the floor. It bounced once, then rolled into Ashley's room.

"Who's there?" Ashley called sharply.

"It's just us," Rose muttered, stepping into the doorway.

Ashley scowled. "What are you two doing here? I hope you weren't eavesdropping on me."

"We weren't eavesdropping, Ashley," Alison said. "We were on our way to Laura and Amy's room to play a trick on them."

"We heard you crying, and we wanted to make sure you were okay," Rose added.

Ashley stared at the cans of whipped cream in the girls' hands. Rose saw that her eyes were red, and crumpled-up tissues lay all over the floor and bed.

"Thank you for your concern, but I'm perfectly fine," Ashley said, turning away so Rose couldn't see her face. "I came back to my room early to read, and..." All at once Ashley's voice cracked, and she reached for the box of tissues.

Sympathy washed through Rose and Alison. They crossed the room and sat beside Ashley on the bed. "What's wrong, Ashley?" Rose asked softly.

"It's my—" Ashley stopped to wipe away the tears spilling down her cheeks. "—my father. Today is my birthday and he completely forgot about it."

"Maybe he'll remember tomorrow and try to get in touch with you," Rose said, trying to cheer her up.

Ashley shook her head. "You don't know my father," she retorted. "*Earl* Worthingham is much too busy with his duties to remember his daughter's birthday."

Earl Worthingham! Alison thought. Oh my gosh. Her father really is an earl!

"Father is traveling in Spain this year," Ashley was telling Rose. "Last year he forgot my birthday because of an important conference. The meeting was in London, but he didn't even bother to visit me at school."

"What about your mother?" Rose asked. "Doesn't she remember your birthday?"

"My parents are divorced, and Mother lives in New Zealand," Ashley replied. "I know that they love me, but all my father seems to think about are his business associates and his social engagements. I haven't had a proper birthday celebration since I was five years old."

Alison and Rose exchanged glances while Ashley leaned over to yank another tissue from the box.

Poor Ashley, Rose thought. She couldn't imagine how she'd feel if one of her parents forgot her birthday.

A few minutes later, Rose heard the corridor outside fill with noisy chatter.

"Everyone's back. We'd better get to our rooms before we get in trouble with Mrs. Stonebridge," Rose said.

"I hope you feel better, Ashley," Alison said, standing up.

"Thanks," the British girl mumbled.

Rose and Alison walked slowly back to the other end of the corridor. Rose was lost in her thoughts. Since they'd arrived, Ashley certainly hadn't been very friendly to anyone. But still Rose felt sorry for her, now that she knew more about her.

The others were waiting in Keisha and Alison's room.

"You guys took forever!" Keisha exclaimed.

Megan immediately noticed their solemn expressions. "What's the matter?" she asked.

Rose and Alison dropped the cans of whipped cream on Keisha's bed and sat down. Together they told the others about Ashley's famous but selfish father.

"So Laura and Amy were telling the truth about that," Rose said.

"My father never, ever forgets my birthday," Megan said. "No matter where his news assignments are, he calls or sends me something. I bet your dad doesn't forget, either, does he, Heather?"

"Once he even called from the plane because he wouldn't be landing until the next morning," Heather said.

Keisha nodded. "My father always makes a big fuss about all our birthdays."

"Mine, too," Alison said. "The year I turned six, he dressed up as 'The Amazing Mr. McCann,' and did magic tricks."

"I remember that!" Megan said, laughing. "You started crying because 'The Amazing Mr. McCann' accidentally made all your birthday presents disappear!"

"You know what?" Rose said suddenly. "Maybe we should do something for Ashley."

"Like what?" Heather asked.

"Like, have a party," she began. "We could..."

The girls stayed up talking until Mrs. Stonebridge finally knocked on the door and ordered them to bed.

It wasn't until Rose climbed under the covers that she realized something: The girls had been so busy with another scheme, they'd completely forgotten about spraying Laura and Amy's room with whipped cream.

Chapter Seven

"HAPPY BIRTHDAY, DEAR ASHLEY"

The next morning the Magic Attic Club girls sprang into action. As soon as they'd finished eating breakfast, they made a beeline for the chaperons' table, where Ms. Clarke and Mrs. Stonebridge were still drinking tea and reading newspapers.

"Excuse us," Megan began politely.

"Good morning, girls," Ms. Clarke said.

Mrs. Stonebridge lowered her paper and gave them a stern look.

"May we help you with something?"

"Actually, you can," Megan replied. Quickly, she told them how sad and upset Ashley had been the night before.

"I wasn't aware that it was her birthday," Ms. Clarke murmured. "Ashley is new this year, and I've been distracted by our cruise."

"So, would it be okay if we had a party for her this afternoon?" Alison blurted out.

"Of course," Ms. Clarke said, smiling. "That's a wonderful idea, girls. We can celebrate at tea time."

Megan glanced at Mrs. Stonebridge, wondering if she were as enthusiastic as Ms. Clarke. The older woman only gave a little nod, then returned to her newspaper.

"Carry on then, girls," she said, waving them away.

In the kitchen, Roger was slicing pineapples and mangoes.

"Hello, ladies." He looked surprised to see them. "Is there something else I can get you for breakfast?"

Rose shook her head, then filled him in on the plan.

"How delightful!" the waiter exclaimed with a smile. "I'm sure we can get something under way for Lady Ashley for this afternoon's tea." Immediately, he began making plans. "Let's see, the pastry chef can bake a birthday cake, and the afternoon chef can prepare some cucumber sandwiches and a lovely trifle and…"

Satisfied that Roger had the refreshments well under control, the girls' next stop was the Topaz Room, where he'd told them a woman named Mrs. Owen ran the ship's arts and crafts program.

Mrs. Owen was in her sixties and very kind. She was just as eager to help the girls as Roger had been.

"We have plenty of balloons left over from a project we did on another cruise," Mrs. Owen said. "And I have glitter and sequins and feathers we can use to make birthday banners. And..." She opened the door to a closet and rummaged around the art supplies for a few minutes. "Here it is!" she declared.

"What's that?" Heather asked, eyeing a huge, brightly colored fish made out of papier-mâché.

"It's going to become a piñata," Mrs. Owen replied triumphantly. "Lady Ashley absolutely must have a piñata!"

The girls split up for the rest of the morning so that they could get all the tasks accomplished in time. Heather and Megan stayed with Mrs. Owen to make the decorations. Meanwhile Keisha, Rose and Alison went to spread the word to their classmates and a few crew members: They were having a birthday party for Ashley at four o'clock that afternoon—and it was going to be a royal surprise!

Keisha straightened the collar on her lavender dress, then held her hands above her head so that everyone could see them.

"Shhhh!" She motioned for all the guests gathered on the top deck to lower their voices. "Please, keep it down, everyone. Ashley should be here any minute now."

Obediently, the crowd quieted down.

Heather held her breath as she stood near the doorway, waiting for the guest of honor to make her entrance. Ashley was expecting to attend the ship's regular afternoon tea on the Sapphire Deck. Instead, she was going to discover thirty-two people waiting to surprise her with a special party.

Everything looks so pretty, Heather thought, gazing around with satisfaction. The girls had blown up brightly colored balloons and tied them to lounge chairs. Colorful banners were stretched along the railings. Roger had placed vases of fresh flowers all around the deck. The afternoon sun shone brightly overhead, and a gentle breeze blew off the turquoise sea.

But the best thing about this party, Heather decided, *is that cake.*

The ship's pastry chef had whipped up a huge sheet cake covered with white icing and decorated with colorful frosting ribbons and flowers. Heather couldn't wait to see Ashley's face when she saw the cake.

Nervously, she checked her watch. As she smoothed the skirt of her pink and white party dress, she saw Beatrice hurrying toward the gathering.

"She's coming!" Beatrice whispered frantically.

Everyone instantly quieted down. Quickly, Megan reached for the birthday cake and held it high.

It was so quiet, Heather could hear Ashley's footsteps on the wooden deck. The instant she came into view, everyone leaped to their feet.

"*Surprise!*" the crowd shouted.

Rose's eyes fixed on Ashley's face. As the startled girl took in the scene in front of her, color flushed her cheeks.

"Oh!" she exclaimed. "I can't believe it!"

Rose went over and put an arm around Ashley. "Happy Birthday, Ashley," she said warmly. "Are you surprised, or what?"

"I'm stunned!" Ashley confessed. "For a moment, I thought I was going to faint!" Then Ashley looked at Rose

and Alison. "You two planned this, didn't you? You wanted me to have a birthday celebration."

Alison grinned at her. "We did a great job, don't you think?"

"A *smashing* job," Ashley said, grinning back.

"Happy birthday, Ashley!" Amy and Laura sang out just then. Before Ashley knew what was happening, the two girls showered her with hundreds of tiny, glittering stars and hearts.

"Thanks a lot!" Ashley said. Laura and Amy laughed as the birthday girl hopelessly tried to brush the confetti off her dress and out of her hair.

One by one, the other guests stepped forward to greet Ashley. Music started up as Roger and several other stewards appeared, balancing silver trays of tea sandwiches and cold drinks on their shoulders.

Alison and her friends exchanged a triumphant high five.

"We did it!" Megan exclaimed, gloating.

"We pulled it off!" Rose agreed.

"Of course," Alison said with a grin. "We're the Magic Attic Club!"

"...Happy birthday, dear Ashleeeee....Happy birthday to you!"

Megan and Alison exchanged happy glances as they

belted out the words to the song. Keisha played the piano with everyone gathered around to sing. Ashley stood in the middle of it all, a contented smile on her face.

Roger pushed the dessert cart closer. The cake glowed brightly with one pink candle.

"Make a wish, Ashley!" Keisha called.

Heather watched Ashley think for a second before she took a deep breath and blew.

"Try again!" Heather urged her when she saw that the tiny flame had not gone out. "Your wish can still come true."

But Ashley shook her head, and let Roger wheel the cake away so he could slice it.

"I don't need to, Heather," the other girl said softly. "This birthday, I got almost everything I wanted."

Chapter
Eight

A MAGIC ATTIC CLUB BIRTHDAY PARTY

That was a wonderful party!" Amy congratulated the Magic Attic Club girls as she sank onto Heather's bed next to Laura.

"Wasn't that cake incredible?" Megan said.

"It sure was," Keisha agreed.

"Well, I know Ashley had a good time," Heather chimed in. "She told me that the food was—" Heather imitated Ashley's crisp British accent. "—*nearly* as lovely as at one of her father's parties!"

"Coming from Lady Ashley, that's a real compliment!" Amy said, smiling.

Amy and Laura left soon to get ready for dinner. A few moments later, they heard a knock on the door.

Ashley stuck her head inside.

"Hi, Birthday Girl," Alison called.

"Hi," Ashley said, smiling back. "I just wanted to thank you again for the party."

"You're welcome," Megan said easily.

"It was nothing," Keisha added.

"It was something!," Ashley said. She looked down for a moment. When she looked up again, Megan saw tears shining in her eyes. "It was the best birthday party I've ever had," she went on. "Thank you."

Keisha felt a lump suddenly form in her own throat. The party had meant so much to Ashley—Keisha was glad that they'd decided to plan a celebration.

As usual, Alison tried to lighten the mood with a joke.

"Maybe by your next birthday you'll be better at whacking the piñata!" she told Ashley. "Today you missed that thing by a mile."

"Give me a break, Alison," Ashley teased back. "We don't play baseball in England, so I don't get much practice at swinging a bat."

After the other girls had left to go to dinner, Keisha reminded everyone that they'd better get ready, too.

Rose groaned. "I'm still stuffed with birthday cake."

"Me, too," Keisha admitted.

"That makes three of us," Heather added. She looked at her friends. "You know what, guys?" she said suddenly. "I think I'm ready to go home."

"I love it here," Megan said. "But I'm ready to go, too."

Within a few moments, the five of them were standing in front of the full-length mirror on the back of the closet door.

Megan looked at the porthole over the beds. Outside, the sun was setting above the blue sea.

Good-bye, *Jewel of the Sea*, she thought with a pang. Then she looked into the mirror and returned home to Ellie's attic.

Rose and Keisha folded their dresses and carefully placed them on top of the white shoes that Alison had worn. Now that they were back home, Rose's thoughts turned to what had been bothering her and her friends before their trip to the attic.

"Okay, everyone," she said. "Ashley's party was a big success—now, we've got to come up with something just

as good for Ellie."

Keisha nodded. She sat cross-legged on the Oriental rug, thinking for a moment.

"Maybe we should forget the idea of a party and buy her a nice present."

"We have almost ninety dollars," Megan reminded them.

"How about a silk scarf from that new shop in town?" Rose suggested.

"Sounds good to me," Keisha replied.

Megan and Alison nodded, too.

"I'm sure the shop is open tomorrow. I'll ask my mother to drive us over in the morning," Rose said.

As the others nodded, Rose realized that Heather seemed hesitant. "Is that idea okay with you?" she asked her.

"I guess, but..." Her words trailed off for a second. "I'm not sure that's what Ellie would really want," she finished.

"But Heather," Alison protested. "Ellie loves scarves. She wears that blue one all the time."

"I don't mean that, Ali," Heather said. She stopped to think for a moment about what she did mean. "I can't really explain it, but after Ashley's party, I'm just not sure about throwing a big party for Ellie or buying an expensive present for her."

"I don't get it, Heather," Megan said puzzled.

"I think I do," Rose spoke up. "What's most important is spending time with Ellie and celebrating her birthday together. That's what Ashley wanted most," she reminded her friends. "She just wanted her dad to remember her birthday."

"Exactly!" Heather said. Rose had said just what Heather had been thinking but couldn't express.

There was a long pause as the others thought it over. Then Alison sat up.

"I have another brilliant idea!" she announced. "Instead of a country club party, we can have a Magic

Attic Club party—just for us, the members of the Magic Attic Club and Ellie."

"That is a good idea, Alison," Keisha said, giving her a high-five. "We can even have it right here in the attic."

"Maybe we can make a scrapbook of letters about our favorite adventures," Megan said. "That could be our gift. She'd love reading about all the adventures we've had."

"We can decorate the attic while Ellie's away, then surprise her with the party when she gets back," Rose said.

The girls decided that Alison would ask her mother to help them bake a cake. Tomorrow they would meet at Heather's to get started on making decorations.

"This all sounds great," Keisha said, jumping up. "But first, we'd better get downstairs to feed Monty his dinner."

While her friends went downstairs to get Monty's food, Heather stayed behind to close the trunk and turn off the light. As the room went dark, she stood alone for a moment, smiling. Soon the attic would be lit up again—this time, with the candles of their friend's birthday cake!